The WISH LIBRARY

Together Forever

The WISH LIBRARY

Together Forever

Christine Evans

illustrated by Patrick Corrigan

ALBERT WHITMAN & COMPANY
CHICAGO, ILLINOIS

For my parents, who always
encouraged my love of libraries—CE

To Dulcie—PC

Library of Congress Cataloging-in-Publication
data is on file with the publisher.

Text copyright © 2021 by Christine Evans
Illustrations copyright © 2021 by Albert Whitman & Company
Illustrations by Patrick Corrigan
First published in the United States of America in 2021
by Albert Whitman & Company
ISBN 978-0-8075-8745-4 (hardcover)
ISBN 978-0-8075-8746-1 (ebook)

Printed in the United States of America
10 9 8 7 6 5 4 3 2 1 LB 26 25 24 23 22 21

Design by Aphelandra

For more information about Albert Whitman & Company,
visit our website at www.albertwhitman.com.

Contents

CHAPTER 1

Duet Trouble

"Attention, Lincoln Elementary!" said Principal Dawkins, his voice booming over the speakers as students lined up outside their classrooms before the first bell. "Our end-of-year talent show is just around the corner. I can't wait to see your performances!"

Raven Rose and Luca Flores grinned as they stood together in line. They knew exactly what they were going to do.

"Soccer skills!" said Raven. She hopped up and

down as if she were bouncing a soccer ball.

"Ballet!" said Luca at the same time. He put his hands and feet in first position and bent his knees up and down, creating a perfect plié.

The two friends stopped and stared at each other.

"What?" they said.

"I thought we could show off our soccer skills as a team!" said Raven, crossing her arms.

"Well, I thought we could perform a ballet duet," said Luca, putting his hands on his hips.

The bell rang, and Luca and Raven followed the rest of Ms. Earl's class into Room 23. Their teacher smiled from the front. "I know you are all excited about the talent show, but let's sit down and take attendance before we discuss it," she said.

Luca and Raven sat side by side at their shared desk but did not speak. Ever since Luca had moved to town, the two had been in sync. They both liked hanging upside down from the monkey bars at recess. They both loved frozen yogurt (any flavor, but especially chocolate hazelnut). And, like all best friends, they shared a secret.

They knew something no one else at Lincoln Elementary knew: In the woods behind their school was a secret place called the Wish Library. Inside, the Librarian and her bearded dragon, Sebastian, kept watch over hundreds of rows of bottles, test tubes, and chests. Each one contained a wish that only library members could borrow.

The problem was, the wishes didn't always turn out as expected. Raven's first wish, for school to be canceled, had led to a snowstorm that closed down the whole town and left the Lincoln Zoo's animals in danger. Luca's first wish had turned him into Principal Dawkins for a day and had almost ruined his friendship with Raven. She was still a little upset that he had gone to the Wish Library without her—and that he'd made a wish without thinking about the consequences.

"Sign-up sheets are posted on the notice board," said Ms. Earl after she'd marked everyone present. "Does anyone want to share what they are going to perform?"

Grace's hand shot up first. "I'm going to play my flute!"

Owen called out, "I'm going to do a magic trick!"

"Please raise your hands, class," said Ms. Earl. "Raven, how about you?"

Raven glanced at Luca. He folded his arms and didn't look back at her. "I don't know yet," she said. She decided she would talk to Luca at recess. Maybe they could come up with an act they could do as a pair. Then they could get back to being best friends who did everything together.

"Well, there's still a little more time. We're going to have our first run-through tomorrow after lunch," said Ms. Earl. "Now, open your readers to page twenty-two, and we'll begin our lesson."

At recess, Raven headed to their usual place in the playground, but there was no sign of Luca. Raven felt like she had when her friend Belle moved away. Lonely.

As Raven hung upside down on the monkey bars, she noticed Grace and Felicity crawling around under one of the chestnut trees that marked the entrance to the woods.

Grace waved toward Raven. "Come play with us," she called.

"What are you doing?" Raven asked.

"Looking for hidden treasure," Felicity said.

Raven gulped. She hoped they didn't go farther into the woods and find the golden coin that revealed the entrance to the Wish Library. The coin only revealed itself to someone who truly needed to make a wish. Then the wish-maker threw the coin into a stone well that also magically appeared. Did Felicity or Grace need a wish? Raven couldn't take the chance.

She flipped right side up and jumped down from the monkey bars. Raven looked around the playground. There was still no sign of Luca, so she shrugged and joined in the treasure hunt. At least then she could stop Felicity and Grace from stumbling upon the Wish Library. The last thing Lincoln needed was more people making wishes without knowing what might happen.

After lunch, Ms. Earl passed around the talent show sign-up sheet. "Some of you already filled this in at recess, but we still have lots of slots left. So if you have a talent you would like to perform, please add your name."

Luca got up from his chair and went to sharpen his pencil at the back of the room. Raven took the sheet from Grace and read what her classmates had added.

Grace: Flute solo

Owen: Magic trick

Felicity: Tumbling

Maya: Break dancing

Luca and Raven: Ballet duet

Raven couldn't believe it. They hadn't even talked about what their performance would be! Luca had gone behind her back. Again. He must have done it while she was looking for him at recess.

Raven scrubbed out her name next to Luca's and added a new line.

Raven: Soccer skills

Raven handed the sheet back to Ms. Earl. Luca sat back down next to her, but she didn't look at him.

"We need to..." Luca started to say, but Ms. Earl was introducing that afternoon's work, so he couldn't finish. Raven was sure he was about to say they needed to rehearse their duet. But she was so mad, she didn't think she wanted to dance with him ever again.

Raven didn't speak to Luca for the rest of the afternoon. During PE, every time Luca came near her, she bounced the basketball away from him. And later, in silent reading, she turned her back on him and kept her nose deep in her chapter book.

At last the bell for the end of school rang. Raven hurried out of class and ran to get her bike. Raven and Luca lived on the same block up the hill, so normally they rode together. But today she biked hard so Luca couldn't catch up.

While getting a banana from the kitchen, Raven heard Luca use their special knock on the door.

"Izzy, tell Luca I'm too busy to play, please," said Raven.

"Really? Are you okay?" said Izzy.

"I'm fine. I just don't want to play today," said Raven.

Izzy looked sad, but she left the kitchen to answer the door.

In her room, Raven flopped onto her bed and thought over the day. How could Luca go behind her back again?

CHAPTER 2

Still Friends?

The next morning, Luca biked over to Raven's house to ride their bikes to school together. He was excited to talk about the talent show at last. At the door, Luca knocked their special knock. *Rat...a-tat-a-tat!*

"Oh, Luca!" said Raven's dad. He looked surprised as he opened the door.

"Is Raven here, Mr. Rose?" asked Luca.

"No, she went to school early. I presumed she was with you!" said Raven's dad. "Izzy is ready though,

11

so maybe you could walk with her and Phoebe?"

After Luca's sister, Phoebe, arrived, the group left for school. Luca trailed behind, pushing his bike. Phoebe and Izzy were chatting about what to do for the talent show, but Luca wasn't listening. Raven had left without him. They'd cycled to school every day since they'd become best friends.

Outside the classroom, Luca lined up behind Grace and Felicity. Raven was at the front by the door. "Raven!" he called, waving.

She didn't turn around.

"Did you two have a fight?" asked Grace.

Luca felt his face flushing. "No!" he replied. "She just didn't hear me."

Grace raised her eyebrows as Felicity giggled. Just then the bell rang, and Ms. Earl opened the classroom door.

Luca took his usual spot next to Raven. She turned her back on him and looked up at the whiteboard. *What is wrong with her?* Luca wondered. Maybe a game would cheer her up.

So Luca got out a sheet of paper and drew a squiggle. They liked to play a drawing game in class. One of them would draw a squiggle; the other then had to turn it into something. Drawing in class had gotten him into trouble before, so he hid the paper in a workbook before he drew a wiggly line. He passed the paper to Raven.

Raven didn't even look at it. She crumpled the paper up in her hand and passed it back to him. This time she did look at him. Her eyes were narrowed, and she looked *really* mad. Luca could feel anger building in his chest.

Then he thought, *Maybe she's upset I didn't show up for recess yesterday.* He'd had to stay back with Ms. Earl to finish his acrostic poem about kindness. He was stuck on a word for the second *s*. While he'd been there, he'd thought he may as well put his and Raven's names down as a double act so they didn't miss out on a spot. He'd used pencil so they could change the act once they'd had a chance to speak. But now she wasn't speaking to him at all.

At morning recess, Luca looked around for Raven. He would try again to talk to her so they could figure out their double act and update the sign-up sheet. But if she wouldn't talk to him, he'd have to perform on his own. Luca found Raven under a tree with Grace and Felicity. They were gathering acorns, sticks, and leaves.

"What are you doing?" Luca asked.

Raven didn't answer.

"We're making a squirrel house, of course," said Grace. "It was Raven's idea!"

"Raven, can I talk to you about our act?" Luca asked.

"No," said Raven crossing her arms. "I'm not performing with you."

"Why—" he started.

But Grace cut him off. "Can't you see she doesn't want to talk to you?"

Luca turned and ran back to the playground, his eyes stinging. Phoebe and Izzy were sitting next to each other on the swings. Maybe Luca could stay

with them until the end of recess. As he walked over, he saw Phoebe quickly put something in her pocket.

"Why aren't you with Raven?" asked Izzy.

"Yeah, why didn't you bike to school together this morning?" added Phoebe.

"It's nothing. Leave it!" said Luca.

Izzy and Phoebe stared at him.

"Aren't you two best friends anymore?" asked Phoebe, her eyes wide.

"No. We're not," Luca replied. And even though the bell wouldn't ring for another fifteen minutes, he ran back to the classroom.

CHAPTER 3

Sticky Situation

After recess, Raven raised her hand.

"Ms. Earl, can I move seats, please?"

Luca had his hand in the air too.

"Actually, Ms. Earl, I want to move seats," Luca said.

"No switching seat assignments! You know that, Luca and Raven. Now, it's time for music class with Ms. Wood. Maybe some of you can learn a new song for the talent show!" said Ms. Earl.

Usually, Raven loved music class. Ms. Wood

always taught them fun songs and talked about different instruments. But today Raven was not in the mood for singing. She just wanted to go home and cry. She hated not speaking to Luca. But it was his fault for going behind her back *again*. It was bad enough when he made his wish without her after promising not to. This was worse. She'd told him she wanted to do soccer skills for the talent show. Why had he put down their names for a duet without asking first?

As Ms. Wood passed around the instrument box and the class selected shakers, tambourines, and bells, Raven decided to just get up and move seats. Everyone was making so much noise that Ms. Earl probably wouldn't even notice. She stood up. Or at least, she tried to stand up. But it was as if she'd sat in super-sticky bubble gum; she couldn't get off her chair! She tried again. She was stuck!

Raven looked at Luca. He was trying to do the same.

"Are you stuck to your chair?" she asked him eventually. This seemed more important than her anger at him. She was getting worried. What if she was still stuck to her chair when she needed to use the bathroom?

"Yeah! What did you do?" said Luca.

"What did I do? I didn't do anything! Why would I glue myself to my chair?" said Raven. She was really starting to panic now.

Grace passed the instrument box to Raven. There were two shakers left. Luca and Raven each took a shaker.

"Okay," he said. "What are we going to do?"

"I don't know. Let's just get through this class," said Raven. Maybe someone really had put super-glue on their seats as a joke?

Raven and Luca joined in with the class, singing and rattling their shakers together to the beat. Every so often they tried to stand up, but they were still stuck tightly to their chairs.

At the end of music, the bell rang for lunch.

"Okay, class, I will see you straight after lunch for our first talent show run-through!" said Ms. Earl.

The kids filed out one by one. Luca and Raven looked at each other.

"Let's count and try to stand up together," said Luca.

"Okay," said Raven. "One, two, three!"

They jumped up so suddenly that their chairs clattered to the ground.

"Oh my goodness!" Ms. Earl clutched her chest. "Luca, Raven, what's going on?"

"Sorry!" they said. But they were smiling. They were free!

"All right," said their teacher. "But please be more careful next time. See you after lunch."

Raven picked up her chair from the ground. She couldn't see anything strange. She touched the seat with one finger. There was nothing there. She saw Luca do the same.

"That was so weird," Luca whispered as they gathered their lunch bags.

"Yeah. Anyway, I'm meeting Grace and Felicity for lunch," said Raven, walking out of the classroom. As she walked, she felt a tug as if someone had pulled her backward.

"Quit it," she said. She wasn't in the mood for games.

But when Raven turned around, Luca was several steps behind her. *Weird*, she thought. Still, she didn't want to talk to Luca about it. She hadn't forgotten what he'd done.

In the cafeteria, Raven waved at Grace and Felicity and ran toward them.

"Oh, I didn't realize he was coming too," Grace said to Raven, pointing behind her. Raven turned around. Luca was still right behind her.

"Um, he's not," Raven told Grace. She turned to Luca. "I'm still angry at you!"

"I know," said Luca. "Can we talk about it later? There's something else..."

Raven wasn't listening.

"Why did you put our names down without asking me? I don't want to do a ballet duet," she shouted. "Now, stop following me."

"I am not following you!" Luca said back. "Can I please talk to you a second? It's about...you know what."

Raven whispered to Grace, "I'll be right back."

Grace rolled her eyes as Raven walked slowly back to Luca.

"I couldn't help following you. I felt like I

was getting pulled behind you!" Luca whispered. "When you ran, I ran too."

"What?" said Raven. "Why are you lying to me?"

"I promise I'm not!" said Luca. "I'll walk away from you, and you can see for yourself."

Luca turned and walked back toward the classroom. After he'd gone a few paces, Raven felt a pull, like an invisible string was attached to her, and she started following him. She couldn't stop her legs from moving!

"You see?" said Luca. "Does it seem sort of *magical* to you? First we were stuck to our chairs, and now this."

"Have you made another wish?" Raven asked loudly. Surely he wouldn't have gone to the Wish Library without her again, would he?

"No!" said Luca, glancing over at Grace and Felicity. "Shhh! I have not!"

"We need to have lunch and get through the talent show run-through. Then we can figure it out," said Raven. "Come on."

"It's not like I have any choice!" said Luca.

As they ate their lunches, Raven noticed how Luca seemed to take a bite of his sandwich at the exact same time as her. And he sipped from the straw of his milk carton when she did. And crunched his apple completely in sync with her. Grace kept looking at them like she was watching a soccer ball being passed between two players. But Grace and Felicity were the least of Raven's worries.

How are we going to get through the talent show run-through? she wondered.

CHAPTER 4

Duet Disaster

After lunch, Raven and Luca made their way to the cafeteria for the talent show run-through. Ms. Earl sat on the stage with her legs dangling over the edge.

"I am so excited to see you all here!" she said, clapping her hands together. "Ms. Wood is here to provide our musical accompaniment."

Ms. Wood stood up from the piano and took a little bow. Luca looked around as everyone clapped for the music teacher. There were kindergartners, like Phoebe and Izzy, and lots of fifth graders too.

Luca suddenly felt nervous about performing his ballet in front of so many older kids. Especially since he wasn't performing a duet with Raven, like he'd planned.

"First, we have Grace, playing her flute!" said Ms. Earl.

Raven and Luca watched as Grace got up and performed her piece. She messed up a few notes, Luca noticed. But when she was done, he clapped along with Raven and everyone else. He hoped the others would do the same for him.

A few more acts performed. Then Ms. Earl called Raven's name. Raven took her soccer ball out of her bag and stood up. So did Luca. She walked to the stage. Luca did too. Ms. Earl's forehead was creased in confusion.

When Raven nodded at Ms. Wood to start the music, so did Luca. Ms. Wood played as Raven warmed up, bouncing the ball on her knees. Next to her, Luca started raising his knees as if he was bouncing a soccer ball too. He couldn't help it!

The kids watching giggled. To them, it looked like Luca was pretending to copy her as a joke. Then Raven caught the ball and started bouncing it on her head. Luca did the same, like a mime. The audience's giggles were roars of laughter now. Luca noticed Grace and Felicity were laughing particularly hard.

Luca couldn't work out what was happening. It was like he was being forced to do whatever Raven did. And something was making them stick together no matter what.

Raven dropped the ball and ran off the stage. Luca was right behind her.

"Why were you copying me?" Raven shouted, tears in her eyes. "Just because I didn't want to do the ballet duet, doesn't mean it's okay to embarrass me!"

"I'm sorry!" said Luca. "I couldn't help it! I had no control over my arms and legs, just like I couldn't help following you earlier."

Luca had wanted them to perform together, but not like this.

"It doesn't make any sense," said Raven, wiping her tears away.

Luca wiped his face too. "I was thinking the same," he said.

Luca raised his arm in the air and waved.

Raven waved too. "Let's try something else," she said.

Luca hopped on one leg. Raven hopped too.

"Right," said Luca. "So we can't get too far apart. We can't move seats away from each other. And we copy each other. What kind of wish is this?"

And what if we are still stuck together at bedtime? he thought.

Raven's eyes were still wet, but she took a deep breath. "I don't know. But I guess we should get back so you can do your act. Otherwise you won't get to be in the show at all."

"Are you sure?" said Luca.

"Yeah. And I suppose you are getting what you wanted," said Raven. "We'll be performing a ballet duet."

"I really didn't wish for this," said Luca. He didn't know what he could say to convince her.

"Well, someone did," said Raven. "And when this is over, we need to figure out who."

Back in the cafeteria, Raven and Luca took their seats, ignoring all the giggles around them.

"Just in time. Luca Flores, it's your turn!" said Ms. Earl.

"Let's get this over with," said Luca.

Raven followed him onto the stage.

Luca stood in first position. So did Raven.

He bent his knees and straightened them over and over. So did Raven.

Luca twirled a pirouette. So did Raven.

Luca ran and leaped across the stage in a grand jeté.

So did Raven. Except, when she landed, she fell over and almost crashed into Ms. Wood's piano. Luca stumbled and fell right next to her.

And as before, the whole audience laughed. Luca looked at their sisters in the front row. They

had their heads bowed, but Luca could tell they were crying. It was sweet of them to be upset for their older siblings.

"Are you okay?" asked Luca. As he stood up, he pulled Raven up with him.

"I'm fine. Sorry I messed it up," said Raven.

"Don't worry. Let's get off the stage," said Luca.

"Luca! Raven!" called Ms. Earl after the auditions were done. "Can I talk to you both?"

They walked over to their teacher.

"What happened up there?" she asked them.

"We...ummm," started Luca.

"We were both a little nervous, so we decided to support each other," said Raven.

"Right. Yes, that's exactly what we did." Luca nodded.

"I see. That's very kind. But you will need to perform alone in the show if you're not doing a double act. It was a little distracting today," said Ms. Earl.

"We understand," Raven said.

"Okay. I'll see you both tomorrow," said Ms. Earl.

"Let's get out of here," said Raven. "And figure out what's happening."

Raven ran to the bike racks, with Luca being almost dragged along behind her. He hadn't realized how much faster she was than him!

CHAPTER 5

Who Did It?

"That was exhausting!" Raven panted as they dropped their bikes on Luca's driveway.

When Luca had ridden in the front, Raven had felt like she was getting pulled up the hill closer to him. When they swapped, she'd felt like she was getting pulled back down the hill instead. Eventually they'd managed to ride next to each other, perfectly in sync.

"Let's get inside and sit down," said Luca. "I need a rest!"

"Chocolate chip cookies?" asked Luca's mom as Raven and Luca sat down at the kitchen table.

"No, thank you, Mrs. Flores," said Raven.

"Are you feeling okay? You always eat my cookies!" said Mrs. Flores, holding her hand up to Raven's forehead.

"I'm fine, just not very hungry," said Raven.

"Maybe later, then. I'll leave them here for you," said Luca's mom. "I'm going upstairs to work for a while. Shout if you need anything."

"We will!" said Luca, standing to give his mom a hug. Raven felt herself rise out of her chair and hug Mrs. Flores too. Luca's mom was surprised, but she gave her a squeeze back.

"Are you super sure you didn't make a wish?" Raven asked

after she heard Mrs. Flores's door close upstairs.

Luca nodded. "I wouldn't lie. Not again."

"Okay, it's just hard to trust you," said Raven. "You keep doing things behind my back. First it was your wish and then putting our names down for the talent show."

"I know. I'm sorry," said Luca. "I only put our names down as a place marker so the talent show didn't fill up! I'd planned to talk to you about what act we should do, but then you wouldn't talk to me."

That made Raven feel a little better. "Okay. Apology accepted," she said. "So what do you think is going on?"

"Someone has definitely made a wish," said Luca, stuffing a cookie in his mouth.

"But why would anyone wish for this? For us to be stuck together, literally?" Raven said once she was done chewing. Despite saying she didn't want one, she'd had no choice about taking a cookie after Luca had.

"Maybe someone wanted to make me embarrass you? So we weren't friends anymore," said Luca.

"Who would do that?" asked Raven. She couldn't think of anyone who would be so mean.

"Well, Grace and Felicity were playing in the woods," said Luca. "Maybe they found the Wish Library. Plus, they were laughing during the talent show."

"They wouldn't try to embarrass me!" said Raven.

"Do you have any other ideas?" asked Luca.

"I don't. But I know who could tell us for sure," said Raven.

"The Librarian," said Luca.

They both grabbed a couple more cookies before leaving the kitchen. As they ran out of

Luca's house, they nearly tripped over Phoebe and Izzy. The girls were sitting on the porch with their eyes tightly shut.

"Ten, nine, eight, seven, six..." they chanted.

"What are you doing?" asked Luca.

The girls looked up and opened their eyes. "Nothing!" Phoebe said quickly. She slipped something behind her back so Raven and Luca couldn't see.

"What's that on your face?" asked Luca, studying his sister. Phoebe's face was covered in red splotches.

"Nothing!" she repeated, covering her face with her hands.

"Izzy, what's going on?" Raven asked her sister.

Izzy looked at her best friend and then looked at her big sister.

"We're so sorry!" said Izzy.

"It's all our fault!" said Phoebe.

"What is?" asked Raven, confused.

"You and Luca being stuck together," said Izzy.

Luca spoke quietly. "Did you two find the Wish Library?"

The girls nodded sadly. They started crying, their tears dripping onto the ground.

"It's okay," said Raven. She sat down next to her sister as Luca sat next to Phoebe. "You can just return whatever wish you made into the test tube."

"We...can't..." Phoebe forced out between sobs. She reached behind her back and pulled out a piece of tissue. When she unwrapped it, Luca and Raven could see that the test tube was inside, but it was broken to bits.

CHAPTER 6

Little Sisters

"Tell us everything," said Luca.

"I found your Wish Library card," said Phoebe. "It was on the floor of your bedroom." She opened her backpack and took the card out.

"Why were you in my room?" shouted Luca. He took the card and stuffed it into his pocket.

"I was looking for your old recorder so I could play it in the talent show," said Phoebe.

"Just tell us the rest of the story," said Raven.

"Phoebe showed me the library card on the way

to school this morning, but we didn't understand what it meant," said Izzy. "We had never heard of the Wish Library."

"How did you find the entrance?" asked Luca. "The wishing well only shows itself to someone who truly wants to make a wish."

"We were upset that you two were fighting, so we went into the woods to talk. We thought if you two weren't best friends anymore, then we couldn't be either," said Phoebe.

"I remembered the library card. So I said, 'I wish Luca and Raven did everything together again,' and then a stone  well and a gold coin appeared. It was just like magic!" Izzy added. "I just knew wishes were real!"

"Then we said the wish again and threw the coin in the well," said Phoebe.

"Because everyone knows you throw a coin in a

well to make a wish," added Izzy.

"We were so scared when we fell down the well!" said Phoebe.

Raven and Luca looked at each other, each thinking of their first visits to the Wish Library. The walls of the well were smooth. It felt like they'd fallen forever in the dark before they had landed on a trampoline at the bottom.

"The Librarian was super scary too. She asked us if we were sure about our wish, and we nodded. We were too nervous to ask her anything," said Izzy.

"I made the wish," said Phoebe. "So she gave me my own library card and a long piece of paper to sign. I couldn't read it all. But what I read sounded bad."

"Those are the consequences if something goes wrong with the wish," Luca explained.

"Well, something did go wrong," said Phoebe. "After you left us on the swings at recess, we made the wish, but we dropped the tube onto the ground."

"And it smashed!" said Izzy. "We didn't know what to do. Recess was over, so we had to go back to class."

"Then these red splotches started showing up on my face," said Phoebe. "I've been cursed!"

"So now we're trying to return the wish anyway, and we hope the test tube will magically repair itself," explained Phoebe.

That's why they had their eyes shut and were chanting, thought Luca. It must have been how they made the wish. But Luca knew that wasn't how to return a wish. To do that, the wisher had to say, "I wish no more, I wish no more, I wish no more," and capture the wish in the tube. If the tube was broken, that wasn't going to work.

"We're going to miss the due date. And face those scary consequences," said Izzy. She started to cry again.

Raven and Luca hugged their wailing sisters and looked at each other. It was time to head back to the Wish Library. Hopefully, the Librarian could help them fix this mess. Otherwise they might be stuck together forever. Or worse.

CHAPTER 7

Back to the Library

Luca and Raven led the way on their bikes, with their sisters behind them on their scooters. They raced down the hill to Lincoln Elementary. Luckily, the gates were still open.

"Come on," said Raven. "We have to get to the Wish Library and get everything sorted out."

In the woods, Luca and Raven stood where the entrance was usually found. There was no sign of it, and no special gold coin. They needed the coin to throw in the well to enter the library.

"What's our wish?" said Raven.

"I wish to end this wish!" shouted Luca. Nothing happened. "I guess that's not a real wish."

"I wish to speak to the Librarian!" said Raven. A coin glinted at her foot. "Got it!"

The four kids gathered around the stone well that had appeared. Raven dropped the coin.

One after the other, the four of them fell down the well. Each knew they would be safe, but they still felt the air rushing from their lungs as they tumbled. Until at last, one by one, they bounced on the trampoline inside the main chamber of the Wish Library.

"Well, well, well, this is quite a gathering!" the Librarian said as Luca, Raven, Izzy, and Phoebe stood up from the trampoline. She was studying a piece of paper and turning a dial on her wish computer. Green numbers scrolled on the dusty screen.

She turned to face them. "You don't need to make a wish to talk to me, you know. You could just call the number on your library card."

Raven hadn't remembered seeing a phone number before. She took her card out of her backpack
and turned it over. It read: CALL A LIBRARIAN:
500-1-LIBRARY. "Huh, good to know," she said.

"So how can I help you?" the Librarian asked.

"Our sisters made a wish," started Luca.

"And they smashed the test tube," added Raven.

"Now we're stuck together!" said Luca.

"We didn't mean for it to go like this!" said Phoebe, clutching Izzy's hand. "We just wanted them to be friends again, so we could stay best friends too."

The Librarian looked at the four kids in turn. They all squirmed under her gaze. Sebastian, the bearded dragon, crawled down from a shelf and took up his usual position on the Librarian's shoulder. He stared at Luca in particular. The Librarian sighed and turned her attention to Izzy and Phoebe.

"You made a wish for Raven and Luca to do everything together again. But the wish computer takes things very literally. I did try to warn you. But you didn't listen," said the Librarian, staring at the squirming girls.

"We're sorry! How can we fix it?" said Phoebe. Her face had even more red splotches now.

Raven looked at Luca, who had turned pale. Luca had told her about one of the consequences of not returning a wish on time. And it was bad. On his last visit to the Wish Library, Luca had noticed how humanlike Sebastian was. The lizard read books, acted as the Librarian's assistant, and even wore half-moon glasses like the Librarian's.

When Luca had asked about the consequences of wishes returned late, she'd hinted that Sebastian had once been a human who'd broken the rules. Raven did not want Phoebe to become a bearded dragon too!

CHAPTER 8

A Timely Solution

"Can we make another wish to fix it?" asked Luca. He started thinking of wishes they could make that would undo what the girls had done. There had to be a way.

"Yes, but you must be careful. Using a wish to undo another is dangerous. Especially when wishes must be returned *on time*," said the Librarian with a wink.

Sebastian crawled back onto the shelf and curled up. Luca imagined what it was like to be a lizard.

He didn't want Phoebe to find out.

"How about we make a wish to break us apart?" he suggested. It seemed to him like the best solution.

"But what happens when we return the wish?" Raven asked. "We'll end up stuck together again."

"How about you wish that we had never made our wish?" asked Phoebe.

Everyone turned to look at the Librarian.

"I'm afraid not. That will create what is called a *paradox*," she said.

"Uh…what does that mean?" asked Luca.

"A paradox is when something can't exist if something else does," said the Librarian.

Luca scratched his head.

"She's saying that if we wish that the girls didn't make their wish, it would be impossible for us to be here right now," Raven explained. "We're only here because they made that wish."

"Right…" Luca still wasn't sure he understood, but he moved on anyway. "So do you have a better idea?" He looked at Sebastian again and gulped.

"I know!" Raven said. "What if we make a wish to go back to recess and stop them from dropping the test tube?"

"Like back in time?" asked Luca. "You can do that?"

Everyone turned to the Librarian, who gave a smile and a small nod.

"If it works," said Raven, "when we return to the present, Phoebe's test tube will still be in one piece, and we can get unstuck."

Luca added quietly, "And no one will get turned into a bearded dragon."

CHAPTER 9

Consequences

"I'll make the wish," said Raven. She knew how terrified Luca was about the consequences of a wish gone wrong.

Raven had her own worries. *What if we end up stuck in the past?* she thought. *There would be two Lucas and two Ravens running around at the same time.* Still, she couldn't think of any other way to fix the mess their little sisters had caused.

Raven had once said she didn't believe in impossible things. She did now. Not only did it turn out that it was possible to make wishes; it was also possible to time travel.

"I wish for me and Luca to go back in time to this morning at ten a.m.," said Raven.

"As you wish," said the Librarian. She punched some keys on the clattery keyboard. More numbers streamed across the wish computer's screen. She turned a wheel and pulled a lever. Out of a printer came a small piece of paper with the shelf location of the wish.

"Stay here," Raven said to Phoebe and Izzy. "And do not touch *anything*!"

"Follow me!" said the Librarian. Sebastian climbed onto her shoulder as she strapped on her silver roller skates. Then she whizzed down an aisle of test tubes, bottles, and boxes. The aisles were too narrow for Raven and Luca to run next to each other, so they followed in single file.

"Slow down!" shouted Luca.

Raven could feel her body being pulled back toward him. But she didn't want to lose sight of the Librarian around the towering stacks of wishes and books. They finally stopped at a door Luca and Raven had never seen before.

"Behind this door are the wishes that can do the most harm. They're even worse than banishments and curses," said the Librarian, looking over her half-moon glasses at Luca and Raven. "Time travel wishes are tricky, very tricky. I don't usually let kids use them. So I'm trusting you to get this right."

Luca and Raven looked at each other. They hadn't had much luck with their wishes so far. They always seemed to go wrong in some unexpected way. Raven had only just returned her first wish on time after tangling with a baby grizzly bear. Luca had become Principal Dawkins to make things easier at school, but he'd only made things a *lot* more complicated. What if they messed this wish up too?

The Librarian placed her hand on a silver panel. Sebastian put one foot on a smaller panel next to it. After the panel scanned their prints, a loud beep sounded. Dozens of cogs whirred until, with a final thunk, the door swung open. The Librarian led them inside a small, dark room. She pulled a

lever, and dozens of light bulbs flickered above them. Shelves full of test tubes, bottles, and chests lined the walls. Some of the chests had heavy chains around them to hold them shut. Luca wondered what other wishes were on the shelves.

"Shelf 208, Restricted Room. These are all the time travel wishes," said the Librarian. "This one takes you back to April 1906, which is best avoided, of course."

"San Francisco earthquake," Raven said to Luca. She'd read a book about it just last week. "What other times do you have?" Raven asked the Librarian. She was imagining being able to travel back and visit scenes from stories she'd read.

"Oh, all sorts, but this is the one you need," she said. "Ten a.m. this morning."

Sebastian took the fizzing test tube from the shelf and handed it to Raven. "Read the instructions, and most importantly, do not get seen by anyone! If you're seen, the consequences will be unpleasant, very, very unpleasant."

As usual, the Librarian didn't explain what that meant. So for once, Raven asked. "What are the consequences of being seen?"

"If someone sees you, you'll become part of their timeline." The Librarian pushed her glasses up her nose. "So you'll be stuck in the past, albeit the very recent past, forever. There will be no Luca and Raven in this version of the world."

Raven and Luca looked at each other. Did they

really want to do this? There was no other way.

Back at the wish computer, the Librarian printed the usual long contract full of warnings and conditions. Raven signed it and handed it back to the Librarian. "How long do we have?"

"When you return the time travel wish, you will be back here just seconds after you left. So you have as long as you need. But remember: make sure no one sees you!"

Luca and Raven walked to the exit.

"Stay here!" Luca told Phoebe and Izzy.

"And be good!" said Raven.

The girls nodded sadly. Phoebe's whole face was covered in splotches now, and Raven noticed her hands were covered too.

"Remember, you will be back here almost as soon as you walk out that door," said the Librarian. "Hopefully."

Luca and Raven looked at their sisters one last time and walked through the exit.

A second later Raven and Luca found themselves on their backs in the woods.

"Come on!" said Raven, jumping up. "Let's make the wish."

Luca read the instructions on the test tube.

TIME TRAVEL WISH

Tip one drop on the tongue of each time traveler.

Then say the time and date of where you want to go.

"Okay. Ten a.m. on Thursday, June tenth. Got it?"

"Got it."

Raven stuck out her tongue, and Luca tipped one drop carefully onto it. "It tastes like your mom's chocolate chip cookies!" said Raven. She tipped one drop onto Luca's tongue.

"Mine tastes like strawberry frozen yogurt!"

The two laughed. Then Raven said, "Let's say the date together. One, two, three..."

"Ten a.m. on Thursday, June tenth," Luca and Raven said.

A tornado erupted around them. They clung to each other as they got swept up inside it and swirled around as if they were in a cotton candy machine. Then they dropped to the ground.

"Did it work?" asked Luca.

"I don't know; I feel the same," said Raven. In the distance she heard the bell ring for the start of recess. They needed to hide before anyone saw them.

"Look, there are the girls!" said Luca pointing to the swings. Raven looked where Luca was pointing. She realized her hand hadn't automatically pointed too. The girls' wish hadn't happened yet, so Raven and Luca weren't yet stuck together.

"Let's hide behind this tree," said Raven. She was just in time, as Grace, Felicity, and

Raven-from-the-past walked to the edge of the woods to play. It was so strange to see herself!

"Oh, there I am," said Luca.

They watched Past Luca walk over to Past Raven. They couldn't hear the conversation, but they both squirmed thinking back to the misunderstanding over the sign-up sheet. If only they had talked to each other, none of this would have happened!

"Now you're going to go to the swings," said Raven. "And a few minutes later Phoebe and Izzy are going to come this way." Luca and Raven stayed still as their sisters ran into the woods and stopped. They talked for a few minutes and then the wishing well appeared. Phoebe threw in the coin.

"And there they go!" said Luca, watching the girls disappear into the well.

A few minutes later, Izzy and Phoebe re-appeared. After they stood up, they read something in Phoebe's hand. *It must be the test tube,* thought Raven.

"I think they're about to make the wish!" said Luca. "We need to be quick."

Luca and Raven crept behind a tree closer to their sisters. The girls had their eyes closed and were counting down from ten. Just like Raven and Luca had seen them do on the porch. Any second now, they would tip the contents of the test tube, and the test tube itself, onto the ground.

"How are we going to grab it?" whispered Raven.

"I have an idea," whispered Luca. "Follow my lead."

Luca held out his hand, and the two tiptoed behind the girls. "Five, six, seven, eight," whispered Luca. Then he spun Raven into a pirouette. She spun toward the girls just as the test tube slipped from Phoebe's fingers. As it fell, Raven stuck her

foot out like she was saving a goal in soccer. The test tube landed on her foot instead of on the dry, hard ground. Raven balanced it like she would her soccer ball. She'd done it!

Now she needed to run before Phoebe and Izzy opened their eyes. Raven carefully lay the test tube on the ground and darted back behind the tree with Luca. Behind her, rainbow sparks flew around Izzy and Phoebe as their wish took effect.

Raven guessed she and Luca would now be stuck together again. She raised her hand to give Luca a high five, and his hand raised at the same time.

"You did it!" said Luca quietly.

"We did it," said Raven, smiling. "Now we need to get back before we're spotted. I don't want to be stuck here!"

When the coast was clear, they ran side by side back to the Wish Library entrance. Luca found a gold coin, and the wishing well appeared. They chanted together, "I wish no more, I wish no more, I wish no more!" and the tornado swept them up.

When they fell to the ground this time, the time travel wish was back inside their test tube, and a sign had appeared over the well that said, RETURN CHUTE. Raven dropped the test tube inside, and down Raven and Luca tumbled after it.

Raven and Luca landed on the trampoline, and Phoebe and Izzy were sitting exactly where they'd left them. To the girls, it had been just a moment since their older siblings had walked out of the Wish Library. The Librarian didn't even bother to look up.

"Did it work?" shouted Luca to his sister.

Phoebe opened her backpack, and there it was, the test tube. In one piece!

"It worked! It worked!" The little sisters grabbed hands and started dancing in a circle. "It worked! It worked!"

"And your face isn't splotchy anymore!" Izzy said to Phoebe.

"Could we stop dancing around my library, please?" said the Librarian. "You're going to break a wish container. And you would need more than a time travel wish to fix that catastrophe."

Phoebe held the test tube and recited, "I wish no more! I wish no more! I really, really, really wish no more!"

Phoebe had to hold the test tube tightly as a mini

tornado erupted around her then disappeared into the tube. Izzy rammed the stopper back in the top, and all four kids breathed a sigh of relief.

"I will take that, young lady," said the Librarian, holding out her hand. Phoebe handed it over, and Sebastian carried it carefully back to its place on one of the towering shelves.

"Are you still stuck together?" Izzy asked Raven and Luca.

"Let's find out," said Luca.

He walked away from Raven. Raven didn't move.

"Phew!" said Phoebe. "I'm never, ever going to make another wish again!"

"Me too!" said Izzy. "Wishes are way too much trouble!"

Luca and Raven exchanged looks. They'd heard that before.

CHAPTER 10

Better Together

The next morning, the Rose kids and the Flores kids met up for their usual journey to school. But now, the four of them all shared a secret.

"Remember, Iz and Phoebe, you can't tell anyone about the Wish Library and what happened," said Raven.

"We won't. We promise!" said Phoebe.

"Did our wish kind of work though?" asked Izzy. "Are you two friends again?"

Luca and Raven didn't answer right away. "Are

we?" asked Luca.

"Yes, I guess we are!" said Raven, smiling.

Phoebe and Izzy cheered and started scootering
to school.

In the classroom, Ms. Earl clapped her hands. "I
am so excited to watch the talent show this afternoon! We have a bunch of talented kids at Lincoln
Elementary. But first, we have math."

The class groaned. They were too excited to
work!

Raven and Luca looked at each other with wide eyes. With everything going on, they still hadn't agreed on what they were going to do for the talent show.

"Settle down, everyone. Let's start on number bonds," Ms. Earl said from the front of the classroom. "If you remember, in a number bond, two parts work together to make a greater whole…"

As everyone was opening their workbooks, Luca turned to Raven. "I have an idea," he said.

"So do I," Raven said with a grin.

The two couldn't discuss their ideas. But Luca had a feeling they were thinking the same thing.

———

"Welcome to our annual Lincoln Elementary talent show!" announced Principal Dawkins from the stage in the cafeteria. The room was filled with parents and kids sitting on lines of chairs. The cafeteria had never been so full. "Friends, your fellow students have worked hard perfecting their acts, and they are ready to impress, so give them your best attention! Parents, we're so proud of your kids. First up, Luca Flores and Raven Rose!"

Ms. Earl nodded to Raven and Luca as they stood up. After they'd told her their new plan, she had agreed to let them do an act together. The parents and kids in the cafeteria clapped politely as Raven and Luca walked onstage. They wore their dance outfits and each clutched a soccer ball. They exchanged nervous glances as Ms. Wood started playing their ballet music.

"Five, six, seven, eight..." whispered Luca. Then they pirouetted at the exact same time before bouncing the balls on their heads five times. Next, they leaped across the stage in a synchronized grand jeté before juggling the balls on their feet. Finally, they placed the balls on the stage and danced around them in perfect harmony. As Luca and Raven finished their performance with a bow, the cafeteria erupted in claps and cheers. In the front row, Izzy and Phoebe cheered the loudest.

"It was so clever of you to combine your favorite hobbies into one act," said Raven's dad after the show was over. "I'd never have thought of putting soccer and ballet together!"

"Celebratory frozen yogurt all round," said Raven's mom. She had made it back from her latest flight just in time to watch their performance.

"Great idea," said Mrs. Flores, hugging Phoebe and Luca. "I'm so proud of you all!"

Phoebe and Izzy had also performed a double act. Luca thought their recorders had been a bit squeaky, but at least neither of them had become a bearded dragon.

Raven and Luca linked arms.

"Chocolate hazelnut?" asked Luca.

"Definitely," replied Raven.

"You know, we make a pretty good team!" said Luca. "When we're not fighting."

"Let's make a pact. If we're upset with each other, we talk about it," said Raven.

"Agreed," said Luca. Holding a grudge had nearly ended their friendship.

"Best friends forever?" asked Luca.

"Forever," said Raven.

A Note to Parents

DK READERS is a compelling program for beginning readers, designed in conjunction with leading literacy experts, including Dr. Linda Gambrell, Director of the School of Education at Clemson University. Dr. Gambrell has served on the Board of Directors of the International Reading Association and as President of the National Reading Conference.

Beautiful illustrations and superb full-color photographs combine with engaging, easy-to-read stories to offer a fresh approach to each subject in the series. Each DK READER is guaranteed to capture a child's interest while developing his or her reading skills, general knowledge, and love of reading.

The four levels of DK READERS are aimed at different reading abilities, enabling you to choose the books that are exactly right for your child:

Level 1: Beginning to read
Level 2: Beginning to read alone
Level 3: Reading alone
Level 4: Proficient readers

The "normal" age at which a child begins to read can be anywhere from three to eight years old, so these levels are intended only as a general guideline.

No matter which level you select, you can be sure that you are helping your child learn to read, then read to learn!

LONDON, NEW YORK, MUNICH,
MELBOURNE, AND DELHI

Project Editor Deborah Murrell
Art Editor Catherine Goldsmith
Senior Art Editor Sarah Ponder
Managing Editor Bridget Gibbs
Senior DTP Designer Bridget Roseberry
US Editor Regina Kahney
Production Melanie Dowland
Picture Researcher Frances Vargo
Picture Librarian Sally Hamilton
Jacket Designer Margherita Gianni

Reading Consultant
Linda Gambrell, Ph.D.

First American Edition, 2000
05 10 9
Published in the United States by DK Publishing, Inc.
375 Hudson Street, New York, New York 10014

Published in Great Britain by Dorling Kindersley Limited

Library of Congress Cataloging-in-Publication Data
Thomson, Ruth, 1949-
    Dinosaur's Day / by Ruth Thomson. -- 1st American ed.
    p. cm. -- (Dorling Kindersley readers. Level 1)
    Summary: A gentle Triceratops forgets to stay with the herd and
has to use his sharp horns to fight a Tyrannosaurus.
    ISBN 0-7894-6635-X (hc) ISBN 0-7894-6634-1 (pbk)
    [1. Dinosaurs -- Fiction.]
    I. Title. II. Series.
PZ7.T38 Di 2000
[Fic] -- dc21   00-027355
                                                        CIP
                                                        AC

Color reproduction by Colourscan, Singapore
Printed and bound in China by L Rex Printing Co., Ltd.

The publisher would like to thank the following for their kind
permission to reproduce their images:
Photography: Dave King, John Downs 14
Illustrations: Simone Boni/L.R. Galante
Natural History Museum: 8-9, 11, 12-13, 14, 15, 21
Ardea London Ltd.: Arthur Hayward 16-17
All other images © Dorling Kindersley
For further information see www.dkimages.com

Discover more at

www.dk.com

DK READERS

BEGINNING
TO READ
1

Dinosaur's Day

Written by Ruth Thomson

DK Publishing, Inc.

I am Triceratops.
I am a dinosaur.
I am big and strong.

Triceratops
(try-SER-uh-tops)

I have three spiky horns
on my head.
I have a bony frill
on my neck.

frill

I look fierce,
but I am gentle.

beak

I spend all day eating plants.
I snip off twigs and leaves
with my hard beak.

I live in a group
called a herd.
We keep watch
for fierce dinosaurs.
They might want to eat us!

All sorts of other dinosaurs
live near the river with us.

Everything is peaceful.

All of a sudden,
what do I see?

A Tyrannosaurus!
He is the fiercest dinosaur of all.

Tyrannosaurus
(tie-RAN-uh-SORE-us)

He has strong toes
and sharp claws.
He has a huge mouth
full of sharp teeth.

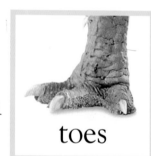

toes

A herd of light-footed dinosaurs
spots Tyrannosaurus too.
They run away on their long legs
as fast as they can.
They hide in the forest.

Ornithomimus
(OR-ni-thoh-MEE-mus)

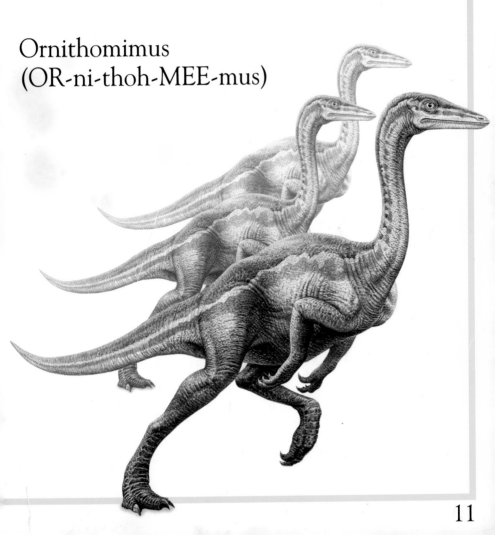

The duck-billed dinosaurs
stop eating.
They watch Tyrannosaurus.
If he comes too close,
they will run away.

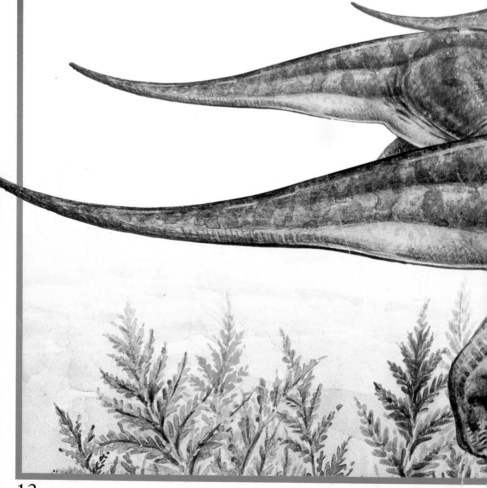

bill

Edmontosaurus
(ed-MON-tuh-SORE-us)

13

The bone-headed dinosaur
looks up and sniffs the air.
He can smell Tyrannosaurus.
If Tyrannosaurus
comes too close,
he will run away too.

Pachycephalosaurus
(PAK-ee-SEF-uh-low-SORE-us)

The dinosaurs with head crests
hoot in alarm.

Parasaurolophus
(par-uh-sore-OLL-uh-fuss)

crest

The armored dinosaur has a club
on the end of his tail.
He gets ready to swing it
at Tyrannosaurus.

club

Ankylosaurus
(an-KIE-luh-SORE-us)

I am busy watching
all the other dinosaurs.
I forget to stay with my herd.

I can see Tyrannosaurus.

He can see me.

Tyrannosaurus runs towards me.
He looks hungry.
His eyes are glinting.

teeth

His mouth is open.
I can see his sharp teeth.

Thud!
Thud!

He comes nearer
and nearer.

21

Tyrannosaurus
stands up.
He is very tall.
He lifts his head
and roars loudly.

Tyrannosaurus is trying
to scare me,
but I am not scared.
I have my sharp horns
for fighting.
I have my bony frill
to protect me.

I lower my head.
I bellow loudly.
Ready, set,
here I come!
Perhaps I can stab
Tyrannosaurus
with my sharp horns.

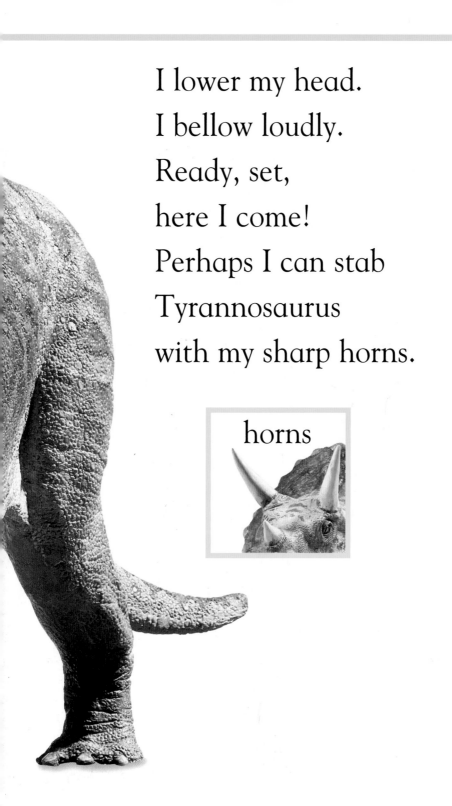

horns

Tyrannosaurus tries to bite me
with his sharp teeth.
I am still not scared.
I kick up the dust.
I try to stab him.

Tyrannosaurus is getting tired.
He stops fighting and turns away.
He goes to look for
a smaller dinosaur
for his dinner.

Now I am safe.

I am going to look for my herd.

I am very hungry
after all that fighting.

I am glad to be back
with my herd
by the river.

The other dinosaurs
come back to the river as well.
They eat peacefully.

I hope Tyrannosaurus
won't come back again.

Picture word list

frill

page 5

crest

page 15

beak

page 6

club

page 17

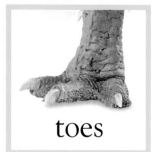

toes

page 10

teeth

page 20

bill

page 13

horns

page 25